PRAISE FOR THE ORIGINAL FRENCH EDITION

"'Literature is the portrait of shadows,' correctly surmises Frédéric Brun, whose first novel strikes its reader by its questioning, its humility, and its necessity."
—ALEXANDRE FILLON, *Livres-Hebdo*

"There is no sadness in this book, just luminous pages, the beauty of well-written phrases, the delicate and pure style of an author one absolutely must discover."
—MOHAMMED AISSAOUI, *Le Figaro Littéraire*

"This book is strong. It seeks no answers, but at the same time refuses to see death as the end of being."
—CLÉMENTINE GOLDSZAL, *Elle*

"Frédéric Brun's first novel begins almost like a fable, startling in its resplendent gentleness when speaking of his mother."
—VALÉRIE MARIN LA MESLÉE, *Le Point*

"This book is a gift that must be given."
—JEAN-LOUIS KUFFER, *24 heures de Lausanne*

"*Perla* is a book that one enters on tiptoes, as one would enter a bedroom still full of a deceased loved one's effects. . . . One holds one's breath in order to hold on to life before it decides to completely disappear."
—CAROLINE MONTREPETIT, *Le Devoir* (Québec)

T0324427

"Simple and clear in its language, yet still capable of spanning a large and complicated subject. Especially when Brun attempts to understand how the same country—Germany—could have produced [both Nazism and] great romantic art. A beautiful book and a glowing bright epitaph. But also—in all its beauty—a defiant act against the great darkness. In all its shapes."

—JEPPE KROGSGAARD CHRISTENSEN, *Berlinske*

"In this tragic but also tender and enlightening tale, Frédéric Brun takes up his pen in order to probe his mother's past and his relationship with her."

—NATHALIE CROM, *Télérama*

"A certain candor adds to the emotion of this debut novel where an adult becomes a child again, who, when confronted with 'the sea of fog' [*mer*], embraces an eternal mother [*mère*]."

—JÉRÔME GARCIN, *Le Nouvel Observateur*

PERLA

Frédéric Brun

Perla

Translated by Sarah Gendron
and Jennifer Vanderheyden

UNIVERSITY OF NEBRASKA PRESS   LINCOLN AND LONDON

Perla was first published in French by Éditions
Stock in 2007 © Frédéric Brun
Translation © 2017 by the Board of Regents
of the University of Nebraska

Cet ouvrage, publié dans le cadre d'un programme
d'aide à la publication, bénéficie de la participation de la
Mission Culturelle et Universitaire Française aux États-
Unis, service de l'Ambassade de France aux É.U.

This work, published as part of a program of aid for
publication, received support from the Mission Culturelle
et Universitaire Française aux États-Unis, a department
of the French Embassy in the United States.

Library of Congress Cataloging-in-Publication Data
Names: Brun, Frédéric, 1960– author. | Gendron, Sarah,
1967– translator. | Vanderheyden, Jennifer, translator.
Title: Perla / Frédéric Brun; translated by Sarah
Gendron; translated by Jennifer Vanderheyden.
Other titles: Perla. English
Description: Lincoln: University of Nebraska Press, 2017
Identifiers: LCCN 2017014279 (print)
LCCN 2017026719 (ebook)
ISBN 9781496202963 (epub)
ISBN 9781496202970 (mobi)
ISBN 9781496202987 (pdf)
ISBN 9781496201027 (paperback: alk. paper)
Subjects: LCSH: Holocaust, Jewish (1939–1945)—
Fiction. | Mothers and sons—Fiction. | Children
of Holocaust survivors—Fiction. | BISAC: FICTION
/ Literary. | GSAFD: Autobiographical fiction.
Classification: LCC PQ2702.R834 (ebook) | LCC PQ2702.
R834 P4713 2017 (print) | DDC 843/.92—dc23
LC record available at https://lccn.loc.gov/2017014279

Set in Ehrhardt by John Klopping.
Designed by N. Putens.

To Véronique, Julien, and Hugo

Death is at once the end and the
beginning—at once separation and
closer union of the self.

NOVALIS

PERLA

PERLA, MY MOTHER, on a beautiful day in 1944, attempted to flee a horde of SS who were chasing her. Once arrested, she found herself crammed into a cattle car alongside other women, men, and children. Upon arrival, she was placed in front of that man named Mengele. In an instant, this elegant doctor determined the destiny of thousands of people. He needed only to extend his hand in one direction. To the right, the crematorium; to the left, the right to live, to hope.

Mengele looked at her briefly. After a quick physical exam, the fate of a prisoner was sealed. Perla suffered from nothing, but a small pimple had burst forth on her face. He hesitated, carelessly extended his hand to the right. She was beautiful. He changed his mind. There is so much indulgence for beauty. He pointed his finger toward the left.

IT'S THE FIRST Saturday of September. Perla spent the summer in the Kremlin-Bicêtre hospital in an attempt to ward off this depression that has been pursuing her for more than fifty years. Leisurely, we have some tea, pick at a few sweets. We head to a bench in the courtyard to talk calmly, our skin caressed by the warmth of Indian summer. As early as next week, I hope to introduce her to Manon, who is going to become the woman in my life. I do not yet know that there will no longer be a next week, Saturday afternoon cakes, a kiss on her forehead, words between us.

At daybreak, Sunday, I immediately understand that the unexpected ringing of the telephone announces terrible news. A hesitant and cold voice devastates me. A bomb explodes in my being, and I scream, crying out to the cosmos. Perla is no longer here.

I return to her final bedroom. Peace has returned to her face. My blood freezes before her motionless body. I kiss her still-warm forehead. Nothing will ever be the same. Where have the billions of souls that came before us gone? I feel as if my mother's soul is within me, and that if I begin this book, it is out of fear that she will otherwise leave forever. While I tap the keys on my keyboard, at times without knowing where these words on the screen are coming from, I ask myself if these hands are really mine or, in some small way, hers.

I go see Perla at the funeral parlor. She is dressed in that Hermès midnight blue suit that she loved so much.

We chose it to please her. She always looked radiant in it. Even more so today. Her face has never looked so peaceful. Some of her wrinkles have even disappeared. She looks like a saint who has been washed clean of everything.

A funeral procession awaits us at the entrance of the cemetery. Our hearse advances slowly. Perla is laid out in the back. Her presence has never before been as strong. From here on, we are destitute, stripped bare, disoriented in the presence of her coffin. Jacques eulogizes her in a moving speech. His notes disappear in the wind.

My mother had never been a practicing Jew. There were four of us in the family. From now on there will only be three. We had to find ten men to recite the Kaddish. Daniel, a close friend, gathers them together, and the prayer is recited in the language of my origins, a somber and harmonious Hebrew. I don't understand the meaning of these words, but they flood me. Once the chant is finished, we head toward the tomb where my grandparents already rest. One after another, we throw a handful of earth. This ritual is really performed for us, the living. Perla is already far away, where she always wanted to be. During her moments of distress, I often heard her whisper, "I want to die." Her secrets, her depression, her moments of beauty remain here on earth.

AFTER MY MOTHER'S death, I lose most of my bearings. Strangely, at the same time I find myself drawn to the German coming-of-age novel, the bildungsroman, and all of its heroes with names of another time: Wilhelm Meister, Henri d'Ofterdingen, Andreas Hartknopf. There are two Germanys. The one of camps and barbed wire contrasts with the one of fog-covered plains, orange sunsets, idealist poets, Novalis, Hölderlin . . . who captured the soul of the world (*Weltseele*). Why am I so fascinated by this country torn between harmony and dissonance, refinement and barbarity? I am astonished to find within it both my favorite literature and the traces of a past that shattered Perla.

When I discover the portrait of Friedrich von Hardenberg, his angelic face fascinates me. In his eyes, a poetic intoxication, a spiritual force embrace the infinite. Yet he died so young. When he met Sophie von Kühn, barely thirteen years old, he fell immediately in love. It wasn't a banal, childhood crush, but the beginning of a metamorphosis. Two years later the young girl passed away, ravaged by tuberculosis. Her disappearance, beyond grief, had an immense influence on Friedrich's soul, as he wrote in his personal journal: "For he who loves, death is a wedding night."

Her burial became a baptism into death for him, a second birth. He assumed the pen name Novalis, meaning "new earth," "soil to be tilled." His quill set out to shatter all boundaries. He created his own space and his own time. He ended his life repeating that he wanted to do so as joyfully as the young poet, the hero of his novel, Henri d'Ofterdingen. Henri, a troubadour in the heart of the Middle Ages, is destined above all else for poetry. This is the key to all of his breakthroughs. In one of his dreams, this sensitivity allows him to open up all the windows of the soul. Through the image of the "blue flower," he senses the resplendent unity of the universe. From that moment on, he will devote the rest of his days to finding it again.

FIG. 1. *Portrait of Novalis*, by Friedrich Eduard Eichens (engraving, 1845). XIR 253260. Bibliothèque Nationale, Paris, France. © Bridgeman Images.

For Novalis, we must be more than men. Our senses allow us to perceive everything, but poetry alone can enable us to go beyond ourselves (*Überbildung*). A cosmic sea lies dormant within, but day-to-day existence separates us from it. Encumbered by interminable accumulations and deductions, the latter leads us nowhere, while the entire universe resides all along in our deepest self.

I no longer like my way of living. The more that time goes on, the more I realize that nothing conforms to how I want to feel. Noise, speed, perpetual technological inventions, the endless search for wealth, individualism, the frantic fight against time—all are becoming unbearable for me. In my day-to-day existence, I no longer perceive anything but uniformity, the pressure to abide by codes, trends—signs of absurd acquiescence. Dissolving into the masses is a way of suppressing loneliness, as if it were always necessary to be plugged in or on the Internet, connected to something or someone. In the great temples of consumption, we amass books and CD-ROMs by the kilo. People want us to believe that knowledge can be bought. Possessing paper objects gives the appearance of being educated. I too want to be connected but certainly not to the shallowness of my era. With his internal voyage (*Gemüt*), Henri teaches us simply to see, hear, feel. By limiting ourselves to what is visible, we only live a partial life. The invisible is nonetheless so close. The living often remain unaware of this. My mother's death is opening new doors for me. My grief forces me to realize that the true path leads within and that Perla is still a part of me. Everything I write leads me to her.

And yet how could Novalis, the German poets, and Hitler's generals spring from the same family tree? The Germanic soul takes us back to nature, to the infinite, to a pure race, to deified beings, to blond hair and blue eyes, to half-nude elves on a quest to find an ideal, an absolute. Victor Klemperer, in *Language of the Third Reich*, analyzes the verb *sich entgrenzen*, which means to destroy all of the boundaries of one's personality, to become one with the universe, to transcend oneself, to break one's chains, to evolve in total freedom. Such notions lead as much to fascism as to romanticism!

ONCE BACK FROM the Polish countryside, Perla quickly realized that its plains of anguish would relentlessly pursue her. Yet in the photos taken on the day of her marriage to André her beaming expression gives the impression that she has erased everything. She was so happy during my first years.

A few weeks after her return to Paris, she went to see a psychiatrist in one of the upscale neighborhoods. In the lobby, she felt out of place in front of that display of opulence, that sofa stretching out as long as her anguish. The lavish ceiling décor and the gold-leafed paneling depicted the sky from a world she had long since forgotten in Silesia. Opposite this famous specialist, she was unable to articulate what was tormenting her. Had freedom bestowed upon her an unremitting, nagging sorrow? She didn't know then that

FIG. 2. Auschwitz. Courtesy of the author.

this anguish would never leave her. She also didn't know that it would mark me, in its own way.

Worried, with so little money on her, she asked at the end of the consultation how much she owed him. The price had to be pretty steep, she told herself, given the luxuriousness of the surroundings and the building. That very sympathetic doctor responded, "Miss, it is I who should be asking how much I owe you." From time to time, pleasant surprises also cross our path.

My mother almost never spoke to me about her deportation. I have to admit that I never asked many questions. I look at the photos she took when she returned to Auschwitz. There are a dozen here. I wonder what she managed to compartmentalize in her memory. Hadn't she hidden things that were best not to disclose? Yet she couldn't erase those blue numbers tattooed on her arm.

I sometimes try to imagine her shaven head, her hollow cheeks, her striped clothes. I had only known her with a full face, dressed in pretty suits or beautiful sportswear. I browse books to identify situations that she might have experienced and end up continuously adding to my library on the Holocaust. In this way, I am reassembling the pieces of a puzzle that she never wanted to piece together in my presence. Was it out of shame, modesty, or a desire to protect me from the atrocities of this world? She would sometimes throw out an anecdote between two topics of conversation, but I believe she did so in an attempt to sever all ties with her cursed year. She was right. Her return was a victory. What she didn't say, too. She succeeded in sketching out for me the path to happiness. She is so beautiful in this role. I am even more aware of it today. Together, we didn't often roar with laughter, but our secret codes and discreet smiles still prevail. In her depression Perla gave up on life; it was her way of externalizing her inability to understand the world. What is there to explain after Auschwitz? What stays with me the most is her illness. I have the impression that my mother expressed herself through it, incapable of revealing what she lived through in any other way, of simply talking about it or writing a novel. The depression was so much clearer than any other mode of expression. She remained there for seven months. How much time does it take to destroy a human being psychologically under such circumstances? One week, one day, one hour?

When I think about all those who traveled through history who were much less fortunate than I—about those men and women with their frozen hands and feet wrapped in multicolored rags—I have real trouble holding on to happiness in my soul for very long. I belong to the new generation of witnesses, the spared lineage, that of the children of the deported. Primo Levi, in his books, speaks of survivor's guilt. It haunts me too at times.

ON TOP OF a rock, like a prince of clouds—hair in the wind, black overcoat, a cane in his hand—a man viewed from behind looks out into the distance. At peace, he appears to have no worries. A sea of whitish clouds seems to envelop the mountain little by little. You can see it extending to the bottom of the valley. From this grandiose display, only a few mountainous fragments stand apart, their color suspended between brown and black. A few pinkish reflections emerge from the milky blue-gray sky. Pine trees obscured by the fog blend discreetly into the background. Silhouette and landscape become one, as if the soul and nature were in perfect harmony. I often contemplate this painting by Caspar David Friedrich. It is on the cover of many books about German romanticism.

FIG. 3. *The Wanderer above the Sea of Fog*, by Caspar David Friedrich (oil on canvas). XKH 141316. Hamburger Kunsthalle, Hamburg, Germany. © Bridgeman Images.

When I observe it closely, I feel a brief moment of serenity. I stare at it while listening to the melancholic notes of today's atmospheric rock. I still have Novalis's words in my head: "I do not know, but it seems to me, that there are two ways by which to arrive at a knowledge of the history of man; the one laborious and boundless, the way of experience; the other apparently but one leap, the way of internal reflection. The wanderer of the first must find out one thing from another by wearisome reckoning; the wanderer of the second perceives the nature of everything."

A majestic maple tree keeps vigil over my PowerBook, asking only to blossom open like a white flower. Trees extend their arms out to mankind, who, profoundly unaware, does not see them. Trees spy on humans, who remain oblivious. Their branches contemplate us, but—imbeciles that we are—we ignore their gaze. The silent light passing between their leaves whispers secrets of the departed. The trees are ready to divulge them to us from the tips of their branches. Birds fly out from them like wondrous words. When I stop writing, I am going to place my hand on Manon's nicely rounded belly. For several months now, I have been expecting a child. I have the impression of being able to feel the universe in the palm of my hand.

ON THE EVENING of the burial, we went for dinner at the Bar des Théâtres with my father and his friend Michel. I am astonished that it's still possible to continue to eat. What can we talk about? The grief is indescribable. However, the menu hasn't changed, and the waiters still take orders with the same good humor. I'm sitting at the table, disoriented. I'm no longer the same. I am no longer her child; have I become a man after all? The street is still lit by its elegant and understated lampposts. André is shattered. We accompany him back to his house.

What could be more absurd than these clothes that are still here, hanging strangely in this neglected armoire; these identification papers that no longer serve a purpose, stored in a crocodile wallet from another time; these foreign banknotes long since discontinued, carefully kept as souvenirs from trips abroad; this agenda where the activities of a swallowed-up day are still written, the appointments traced in delicate handwriting. On her night table, I notice the pocket calculator I gave her one Christmas. I bought it in a drugstore that also no longer exists. How at this point can it help me enumerate all the painful moments I will live without her, all those hours when Perla was sweet, when she was enamored with her beloved child? What to do with all of these high heels strewn about, still unsorted in this armoire; all of these purses, once so chic but now useless? She will never again go anywhere with them.

A type of harsh and sharp silence reigns over the apartment where André decides to live out his final days, that decision slowly killing him. Their love resides in each object, each knickknack. The atmosphere is hard to bear. When I walk through Perla's room, my gaze stops momentarily on a random piece of furniture, on a frame where her sunny face beams; a lump forms in my throat. I have nothing left to say, nothing left to do but stand here, immobile, with all of my thoughts. Thankfully, Manon is holding my hand.

ON THE PLATFORMS of the train station, men, women, and children were struggling in vain against an incomprehensible and pitiless force. In complete confusion, the crowd was panicking amid locomotive whistles and screams. A succession of trains was departing for the cold and the unknown. It was the moment of last contact, the final glimpse of a loved one's face. Mothers were running with their nursing babies in their arms; children thrown to the ground were struck by the steel tips of boots. With torn clothes, they pleaded for mercy under the blows of clubs, and then, heads bowed, they resigned themselves to their fate and climbed into the terrifying cattle cars. The numbers were traced in chalk . . . 150 . . . 200 . . . for more than four years, this scene replayed thousands of times. The trains of deportees departed again and again while the war continued, and the majority of the French knew nothing of these unfathomable nocturnal convoys. I know nothing about Perla's journey. It's through books like *None of Us Will Return*, by Charlotte Delbo, that I am discovering detailed descriptions of departure scenes. How had Perla reacted? Had she screamed out, cried on the station platform? Had she panicked? She always remained silent about her journey to Germany. In those stifling train cars, long, shamefully long, how had she behaved? Had she resigned herself to her fate, or had she revolted upon hearing the doors bolting shut, the orders and screams, the incomprehensible unrest, the noise of signal boxes resonating in the odious night?

Next to her, men were whimpering, pissing, shitting on the straw like animals. The air had become unbreathable. Death rattles flew across the lone ceiling window only to become lost in the great indifference of the countryside. How had she spent the night? Surely she talked about it with other survivors during the reunions of the Friends of the Survivors of Auschwitz. Perhaps she had spoken more about it with my aunt or my father? With me, she had always kept the secret. Oddly, rather than prolonging her silence, I am documenting it. Does any of this make any sense? Why all of this reading? Jorge Semprún's *Literature or Life*, Primo Levi's *Survival in Auschwitz*, Elie Wiesel's *Night*, Simon Wiesenthal's *The Sunflower*, Jean Clair's *Ordinary Barbarity*, Robert Antelme's *The Human Race*. It's a way of keeping her with me. Through writing, I seek the boundary between dream and reality, oblivion and appeasement.

FIG. 4. Auschwitz. Courtesy of the author.

OUR CHILD IS little more than a rough draft. After several weeks, his tiny arms and his miniscule legs are just barely visible. His heart is beating! The embryo begins by creating two cells per second, then one thousand, two thousand, five thousand. He will have sixty billion when he comes out of Manon's womb. As with my wife's womb, I neither understand why nor how all of the characters I type on my keyboard reproduce themselves on a screen and remain etched in the memory of a hard drive, about which I also know nothing, neither the origin nor the composition. Nor do I understand anything about the alchemy taking place in Manon's body, about this great, mysterious, silent construction of the human machine. Everything is becoming an enigma in my mind. Where do the instructions for creating life come from? Where does the voice that dictates my writing come from?

I learn we are expecting a boy. We decide to name him Julien. He still sleeps twenty out of twenty-four hours. Eyelids and eyelashes well defined, eyes closed, he is already able to profit from a multisensory concert. The reverberation of his parents' voices is bathed in a sonorous and fragrant placenta. Auricles already well formed, his ears orient themselves toward these simple and enchanting sounds. He comprehends nothing, neither day nor night. He has the unbelievable good luck not to be inundated by the billions of sensory aggressions to which I am victim each day and lives in something of a sublime world, whose simplicity can connect him to the infinite.

I think about the time when I was in Perla's womb. Of course I have retained no memory of this, and yet I too kicked my feet. I rolled in the amniotic fluid. I moved around in that aquatic and serene universe. It appears that those very months decided how the rest of my life would unfold. I wonder if my child will be totally cut off from this world of yesterday. I also wonder if all of those chromosomes, in the process of constructing him, will retain some trace of the past that forged both my personality and Perla's torments or if they will definitively skip an entire generation.

TWO MEN STAND immobile in the half-light. Silently, they stare at the horizon on a sky-blue beach. Light unites heaven and earth. Time and clouds seem to stop. Undoubtedly, they wish to transcend the reality of the world, to pierce its appearances with their visionary souls. I feel profoundly drawn to this colorful reproduction of unity and the universe. I now think there is only one way to avoid the harmful proliferation of sensations and to purify oneself. It is to be found on the path of renunciation. Sorting or discarding must become a perpetual battle. I take more and more pleasure in stripping myself of everything I don't consider indispensable to my existence. Having everything, I soon

FIG. 5. *Moonrise over the Sea*, by Caspar David Friedrich (sepia wash over pen, 1835–7). BOO 73754. State Hermitage Museum, St. Petersburg, Russia. © Bridgeman Images.

realize I have too much and therefore have nothing. Pruning branches allows for the preservation of a plant's lifeblood.

I also need to conserve my energy, to shield my nervous system by eliminating all useless activities. We gaze upon life too quickly, and we see nothing. In ancient China, a painter would apparently sit for days and months in front of a tree before painting it. In this way, he eliminated the distance separating them. By contemplating it, he managed to become the tree. Only then could he begin his painting.

For the writer to reach the height of his art, to wield words, adjectives, the right verbs, to trace out the fullness of those two individuals walking along the shore, he must have patience.

HUNGER WAS EVERYWHERE. It was becoming an obsession. It entered into glazed eyes, dozed on protruding cheekbones, curled up in each cavity of the body, trickled down along ribs that almost pierced through skin. Because of it, people would fight like animals. The smallest morsel of bread was now the purest jewel. Some would swallow it in one gulp, while others would hide it under their straw mattresses, prolonging the moment of savoring it. Others still would roll it into little balls in order to eat it slowly . . . slowly . . . slowly. They would dream about a second one. How they were going to trade it, steal it, try to find it in the mud. They would lie in wait for crumbs or fruit peels. They would throw themselves on those scraps, today thrown carelessly into our trash cans. They would watch the privileged *Kapos* as they devoured entire chickens. From a distance they would see those cabins, just

FIG. 6. Auschwitz. Courtesy of the author.

barely separated from the camp, where the families of Nazis would shamelessly savor their elegant cakes.

And then there was the insane act, that of going to look for it, at night, in the kitchens, this bit of bread. Several times, Perla dared the impossible. Compelled by an invincible force, she would cross the camp inconspicuously in the middle of the night to steal, like a schoolgirl, that miraculous commodity. She knew what she was risking. She would only take a few pieces so that her crime would remain undetected. In her block, she would distribute it without asking for anything, not cigarettes or soup or anything else in return. Did she embellish this story a little? It doesn't matter. Sixty years later, I am still so proud of her.

JULIEN ENTERS HIS final term. He learns to manage his senses. Little by little, he masters the use of his organs. He drinks from the internal sea of Manon's womb. His little stomach, his little liver, his little pancreas, and his little intestines learn the mechanics of digestion. We are all social beings. In our own way, we all seek to connect with something greater than ourselves. Each of us has his or her own belief system, and my faith resides in connections, those unexpected relationships governing the order of the Milky Way, those ties between life, love, death, sounds, words and colors, art and childhood, the grain of dust and the infinite. These natural intimate connections have remained a great mystery since the dawn of time. In my mind, Perla became an eternal star. It is in this way that I am connected to my writing, to my silent child, to Manon, to my mother in the whispering cosmos. Trees watch this spectacle. There are so many similarities between a tree and a book! The origins of the word *livre* in French, "book" in English, and *Buch* in German are all connected. *Livre* derives from the Latin *liber*, the membrane that separates wood and bark. Once dried, this membrane was able to receive the first written words. This book to which I am giving birth, my son who is taking form, the tree I am watching while writing, all have the same roots.

WE ARE IN the living room, quietly watching television. Suddenly Perla has a crisis and sharp words fly out of her mouth. Insults rain down. André and I are paralyzed by her words. We listen to her without resentment. And then peace returns. Life resumes its normal course.

Such moments were in direct contrast with the woman she presented publicly when all was going well. Once back in Paris, within a few years, she succeeded in starting a business, finding housing in a nice neighborhood, meeting André, having a child, forging precious friendships. The positive road, she knew this too. Beautiful, elegant, she was capable of the best. Full of good intentions, she knew how to be generous. She would wear the top designers, decorate her apartment with refinement. People close to her would compliment her on this. She knew how to be funny, even making light of what had happened to her during her deportation, sometimes daring an off-color joke on the subject, but in the end nothing could be done; the traces of damage were always there. Perla would often stay for hours slumped over in her bed. When she retreated into her silence, nothing mattered. The lowliness of men, hopelessness, time sweeping everything away, old age, wrinkles, the inevitable decline of a seductive woman—everything must have blended together in her dark thoughts. How she must have suffered. In spite of my efforts and those of André, nothing could be done. She had reopened the gates of hell. No one could close them. We would try for few moments to console her. She preferred to be alone. She wanted to die. Is that why her face looked so peaceful, became so calm, so radiant when she closed her eyes for the last time?

SHE SAW THAT roundup take place. She must have crammed herself into the straw in that train. Upon arrival, she must have resigned herself. She was thirsty. She was hungry. She was cold. She had that same bitter wind on her skin. She had that same rain clinging to her clothes. She feared the cracking of the whip on her shoulder blades. She was forced to be naked in front of strangers. She heard those same screams, those death rattles, those futile protests whirling in her ears. She could do nothing other than submit. She felt that fatigue in her failing legs. She felt her knees crushed by stones. She endured that odor of burned flesh in her nostrils. She couldn't wash herself for months, not her body, her face, or her teeth. She ran between submachine gun bursts. She executed orders in that language she was forced to learn. She heard the guards' incessant steps. She dreaded Christmas snow. She was harassed by one of the *Kapos*. She felt beaten in the mud. Diarrhea ran down her thighs. She pressed up against other women during those sleepless nights. She responded to the morning roll call. She heard her number shouted out instead of her name. She stood at attention in front of her block. She walked in rows of five or ten. She paraded before a strange marching band. She was afraid under the bright floodlights. She saw those plains, that snow, that barbed wire, those watch towers. She went to those latrines. She learned the latest news in that place people called "Radio-Crapper." She held out her dish for a little soup. She became thinner from week to week, from month to month. She saw Mengele again in the sick bay. She became a guinea pig for his experiments. She held on. She slept on a stretcher so that she could be sent back more quickly. And then she returned. She remained silent, and I didn't want to know anything about it.

AT THE MAYOL concert hall, near the Rue du Faubourg-Saint-Denis, artists would sing amid young girls, nude and covered in flowers. When the war broke out, it closed down, as did all Parisian theaters. However, the iron curtain was once again raised in many theaters under the control of the *Kommandantur*. Even though they considered its performances to be Western decadence, the Germans authorized the reopening of Mayol. Parisians tried to continue to live normally and, little by little, regain their composure. In spite of their divided country, food rations, fear of a city under high stress, wounds and humiliations, they would seek out a little bit of happiness and oblivion in the cabarets. They would also go there to warm up. At home it was cold, for lack of coal.

André, in the magical time of his twenties, was living the crazy adventure of a life just beginning, full of billions of promises. He was practicing the profession of an entertainer, which he had begun three years earlier. In the Paris of drama and tears, hat tilted back and a flower in his buttonhole, eyes filled with hope and playfulness, he would launch into choruses of Trenet. How good it is to bring a little happiness to people. It takes but the time of a song!

As for Perla, she was living in the south of France. Her best friend, Christine, advised her to return to Paris to take advantage of Parisian life despite the Occupation. Perla could have crossed paths with André in a cabaret or on the

Grands Boulevards, but the course of their destiny had already been written. Perla went for a walk one beautiful morning of that year, somewhere she shouldn't have.

A few months later, crowds invaded the streets and city squares. Security guards were overwhelmed, the fairground stalls were ready to collapse, alcohol was flowing in waves, and all of the loudspeakers were broadcasting the same tune: *Ah, le petit vin blanc, qu'on boit sous les tonnelles*. Everyone was carefree, having the time of their lives, many of them singing those simple and popular words *pour sauter dans les bois, dans les prés*. That song about old romance went well with the jubilation of the Liberation. It's the song that brought André luck.

Far from the fanfare of the celebration, Perla was not yet free and was living her last moments in the Silesian countryside. From the open-air dance halls of the Eastern Front, it was much more than mere miles. Light years separated the extinguished eyes behind barbed wire from those of the free. André and Perla did not yet know each other.

Much later, in the mid-1950s, they met on a patio perched atop the peaks of Haute-Savoie. Under a happy, deep blue sky, without one dark cloud, with the whiteness and purity of snow as a backdrop, chance placed André in front of Perla, who was having lunch alone facing the mountain. Her face, bronzed by the sun, was glowing. André, in a bright red wool sweater, was terribly attractive, filled with a perfect zest for life. She was immediately charmed by his angelic face, his long, delicate hands, and especially by his first words. From that moment on, Perla was quite far from the *Lager* she had known twelve years earlier. That day she erased everything. Love was going to shake up her world for the better. Still today, etched into the depths of my being, I hold onto the magic of their loving gazes.

THE DAY OF Perla's death, a bomb also explodes in Nacha's brain. She has always lived in the shadow of her older sister—the sun of her galaxy—and without her, her life is no longer possible. She suddenly loses all concept of space and time. Those who know her are so sad to see her in this state, but she isn't unhappy; she's floating. In her mind, all that remains are scraps of memories that rarely come to the surface. It's the beginning of daylight saving time. She goes downstairs in her nightgown to walk in the nocturnal silence of her neighborhood's deserted streets. She no longer recognizes familiar faces. She walks in circles in her apartment and seems to dwell endlessly on ideas unknown to the rest of us. What waves of emotion flood over her when she is on the verge of tears? Does she have flashbacks of wild times, agonizing recollections that invade her? If yes, then what colors are those flashes?

As for André, he falls into a pit of despair when my mother's soul departs into space. Hopelessly stuck on earth, the weight of his memories prevents him from lifting his feet to walk into the future.

I often yearn to just close this book of reflections. The concerns of the bildungsroman are a far cry from the preoccupations of today's world. Yet reading Ludwig Tieck's *Franz Sternbald* gives me courage. Seeking fulfillment, Franz leaves Nuremberg. He hopes that Rome's majestic beauty and Raphael's paintings will succeed in transforming him. Along his route, a manufacturer strongly advises him against the career of a painter. He could make a good living by staying there. Franz is astonished that men are so absorbed by wealth. He prefers the company of trees, which console him of the thought of so much baseness by providing the answers to all of his questions. Regardless of others' scorn, nothing will replace his true calling.

I FOUND ONLY one book on the camps in Perla's library: *The Hell of Treblinka*. She had underlined just this one phrase: "Cain, where are they? Where are the people you brought here?" What became of those piles of stolen hair? In which ropes of the German fleet were they used; did they still flap in the wind? In order to recycle as much as they could, they would extract gold teeth! What have they adorned since? They made soap from corpses. So who washed with it? Only ashes remained, transported in farm carts, dispersed across fields like a great black tide. They took flight in the north wind, dusting the surrounding plains. Trees continued to grow in Birkenwald. They are now tall.

I immerse myself once again in the blessed time when Perla was still around. At that time, I found her presence normal. Now, I understand that this presence had really been exceptional and that I should have taken advantage of it more. Like Hyperion, I am seeking an era that has been definitively swallowed up. For him, our sole aim should be to find the beauty and unity of the world, the golden seed from which we all spring. Friedrich Hölderlin relates the turmoil of that torn being who dreams of nothing "but to be one with all living things, to return, in radiant self-denial, into the All of nature." Distraught, Hyperion struggles endlessly as nature does not open her arms to him. By taking the path of divine Antiquity, he hopes to rediscover the infancy of man and inner peace. But, if man seeks beatitude, it's a quest destined to fail. We are like that dead leaf that hopes in vain to climb back upon the tree from which it fell.

There is nothing surprising about the fact that Hölderlin's messages were appropriated by the Third Reich. The condemnation of petit bourgeois capitalism, the return to the sacred and to nature, and the conception of a Germanic Hellenism are the major themes of National Socialism. From the Hellenia dreamed of by Hyperion to the great Germania, where man is in perfect harmony with his surroundings, people, and God, there is but one step. The most beautiful poetry could thus be absorbed by the worst tyrannies. What should one think about this German romanticism, pure and doubled? Words have their idyllic side and their diabolical side. How is it that, a few feet from the crematorium ovens, the SS were able to listen to the quintessence of German music, the divine harmonies? How could Hölderlin's language blossom on Hitler's lips? How could words that used to express a magical and eternal poetry become so harsh, so sharp, and so cruel? Behind the barbed wire, there is Jena, the Athenaeum, fragments, absolute romanticism, the Schlegel brothers. Cruel separation, parallel worlds! What is there to learn from the Holocaust? The devil is within man, but did good ultimately triumph over evil? I am a post-war child. People fought so that I could avoid this disaster and live in the free Europe of today. I can count myself lucky.

FIG. 7. *L'enfer de Treblinka*. Courtesy of
the author.

Man is so complex. He can be refined, cultivated, and
animalistic at the same time. There are two Germanys
because there are two sides to man. The man who conceived
of crematorium ovens is capable of savoring petits fours at
a dinner buffet while in his elegant uniform, wooing the
most charming women, and reading poetry in a well-made
bed. The man who can cold-bloodedly shoot a bullet into
the temple of his fellow man is capable of being impas-
sioned about other human beings, of pledging to them

his faithfulness and loyalty. Duality. You make the world dance to the music of the Uncanny (*Unheimliche*). How could humanity produce both Auschwitz and Novalis? I've examined this question from every angle, but I still find no answer. No one can answer it. We are made to be confronted by contradictions: our contradictions.

FIG. 8. *Portrait of Hölderlin*, by F. K. Hiemer (pastel). XRD 1729002 © Bridgeman Images. All rights reserved.

IN 1949, Josef Mengele fled Europe for Argentina. He then moved to Brazil. The man who had dreamed of a new civilization that would last a thousand years, of a pure race of white, blond men, ended his life in the midst of miserable wooden shacks. Between several shanties where children played, he lived like a simple retiree, a satellite fallen on a lost continent. There, anonymous and respected, he succeeded in escaping the hellfire of current events. He did his shopping and cleaned his house. In his living room, a television broadcast images of the world from which he had fled.

I try to imagine the end of that man's life, the one whose gaze Perla had crossed before. Mengele drowned in a pool even though he was a good swimmer. No one knows the exact circumstances of his death. Did he escape again? Such a mysterious and elusive man! Did Mengele commit suicide? Did he die by accident? What remains of the angel of death? A skull, some bones at the forensic institute of Sao Paulo, abandoned by his family? Why had he told Perla to go to the left? Who knows the answer? At the Yad Vashem museum in Jerusalem, the Avenue of the Righteous is lined with young trees nourished by water from the river Jordan, planted in memory of all of those Gentiles who saved Jews during the Holocaust. What do these trees think about while growing? I remain like Perla, lost in the haze with no answer. She often seemed to be elsewhere, far from those closest to her, isolated in an incomprehensible world. They are still here, traces of the Holocaust, in my personality, in my behavior.

JULIEN JUST FINISHED his first seven months in flotation. He is still eight weeks away from being born, as we start counting a child's age at the moment of birth and not in utero. He is about forty centimeters long and weighs one kilo and seven hundred grams. It is while approaching the end of his hibernation in Manon's round belly that he grows the most. By the time he leaves the amniotic liquid, he will have doubled in size. I am writing more and more as Julien's limbs grow exponentially from day to day. While my fingers graze the keys of my keyboard, the nails and hands of my son begin to develop. As his body wedges into the uterus, sounds reach his ears more directly. Cramped in his capsule, he places himself little by little into his definitive position.

By the time my son leaves Manon's warmth, the temperature of the outside world will drop to around thirteen degrees Celsius. I am afraid to let go of my illusions. Must I really finish my book so quickly? Through writing, I still keep a little of Perla with me.

I dive into Karl Philipp Moritz's *Anton Reiser*. This character dreams of becoming an artist. As an adolescent, he has a fervent hunger for reading. Nourished by Virgil, Goethe, and Shakespeare, whom he admires to the point of depriving himself of simple worldly nourishment, he then navigates from defeat to defeat and, despite an indestructible will, never manages to climb the rungs and attain the successes to which he aspires. Victim of a failed education, of a mind at odds with reality, he spends his time searching.

His apprenticeship does not allow him to blend into society. Alone, he finds refuge in reading, which offers him some compensation. He thus attains a state of well-being by permitting himself to be cradled by his desires. For Anton Reiser, there is some joy in knowing that others consider him accomplished, or at least that he passes for it. That's enough. I am also there, curled up in my bubble of poetic prose that keeps me intact. *Die Einbildung* is imagination transformed into chimera. Am I not often its victim?

PERLA WAS BORN in Olkusz, near Kraków in Poland. She emigrated to Paris and ended up in the Jewish neighborhood of the Marais. When she was brought to Oświęcim, she was simply coming back to her country of origin. In that village called Auschwitz, in the countryside of her native land, she was considered a foreigner. In fact Perla had not been expelled from a precise territory; she had simply been deported outside of the borders of humanity. When she arrived there, she was forced to undress. That was her first humiliation. They showered her. They tattooed her. They shaved her. They decided to replace her name with a number. They even conducted experiments on her that would seriously restrict her chances of one day having a child. Upon returning she had to really fight to become a mother. What more is there to know? I wonder why I have such a need to immerse myself in her story. I have the impression, through writing, of rebuilding a bridge between her and me. But what do I really know about her? For me, Perla remains a mystery. She never really knew me either. We didn't take advantage of our time together; there was too much barbed wire between us. I am going to the Holocaust Memorial, a few steps from the maid's room where she lived with Kopel, her father, Nacha, and Mayer, her older brother. I look for her name. It is inscribed on the stone. I find a Perla, but I chose the wrong wall. It wasn't her. There was another Perla! What became of her? Did she survive? My heart is beating faster. How many Perlas are etched into this marble? A little farther along, I finally find the right inscription. The first concrete trace of her deportation is there, in front of me. It's not much. A few gilded letters. There are thousands of names. I remain fixed on yours, Perla, a little surprised to be here in this strange situation, at once so anecdotal and so powerful.

JULIEN FINISHES THE two hundred and twenty-three days of his cozy cruise. Cramped in a capsule that is now too tight, this bit of flesh called a fetus must complete the voyage. In the dark of night, Manon feels her first contractions. We travel across the sleeping city to the maternity ward. It takes Julien but a few minutes to eject from his cockpit. He arrives wrinkly, sticky, and covered in blood. He has made an epic trip within the space of a few short minutes, the greatest ecological move there is. He has passed from the aquatic world to the "erratic" world. Odors, tastes, sounds, all of the parameters of his universe have changed, and his transfer from one world to the next ends with an immense scream. I let out exactly the same scream when I learned about Perla's death. Everything begins, everything ends with this scream—writing, life, birth—as if on our earth there is something unbearable that each of us seeks to express in his or her own way. The fetus who becomes an infant dies while being born, is born while dying in the time of one respiratory explosion. Julien experienced, like all newborns, the feeling of imminent asphyxiation.

After his planetary relocation, Julien recognizes his mother's familiar voice, but her enchanting siren's song does not shield him from the great shock of earth and oxygen. Disembarking into a blindingly bright light, into air that is too heavy, his lungs begin to inflate and deflate with great, jerking movements. Little by little, the music of his parents' voices reassures him. He discovers the vibrancy of our eyes. He has left the internal night, and we are as invisible as angels. From this point on, we are even more present for him; we have become the closest lights, sounds, and smells.

By accident I discover *Lucinde*, the novel by Friedrich Schlegel, in a bookstore. Julius endlessly laments being nothing but a fragment of himself until the day he discovers great love with Lucinde. We live an incomplete existence instead of being in tune with the boundlessness of the universe. The majority of men live in a mediocre way, like the *Teilmenschen*, a term employed by Hölderlin in *Hyperion*, meaning fragmented men. Preoccupied with their day-to-day concerns, they cut the vital cord that links them to the essential. Full of simple-minded, crude enthusiasm, they completely lose the meaning of the divine. Prometheus leads them down the path of effort and competition, while sublime idleness would have allowed them better to profit from existence. It is thus that people from the North lose themselves by following his call, unlike those from civilizations of the ancient Orient, who live much more harmoniously. It is only through tranquility and gentleness of character, in the sacred calm of passivity, that one can have a memory of one's total self.

Julius suffers for many years. He falls ill and decides to gamble away his possessions. He claims to be an artist, but his paintings and sculptures are cold and devoid of grace. This great love he shares with Lucinde is going to revolutionize his life. She is going to be the extension of his fragmented self and allow him to once again find the all-encompassing beauty of the world. From then on, his paintings take on life and are filled with a beautiful light, the reflection of his internal life. Where he used to struggle for hours, now he achieves everything spontaneously and effortlessly. His work finally finds the path of truth. Schlegel's thoughts concur with those of Novalis. The resemblances between the two poets are numerous. Julius, however, has a more earthly side. He discovers fatherhood and retains a social connection.

I met my Lucinde. Manon metamorphosed my existence. She is the source of all of my happiness. She gave me a child, made the words of my book surge forth, and taught me to look at trees. What more can I ask of life?

AUSCHWITZ IS PART of my life, even though I was never there, even though my mother survived it. Auschwitz is a small part of my DNA, but neither a greater nor lesser part than my father's optimism, than all of life's gifts I have received. When I say "Auschwitz," I should say "Birkenau," the women's camp. I look for it on a map.

Little more than ten barracks make up this block. They were built without foundations, directly on marshland. Which barrack was she in? Divided into three levels of bunks per barrack, the block contained sixty-two alcoves.

FIG. 9. Birkenau plan. United States Holocaust Memorial Museum. Courtesy of the National Archives and Records Administration, College Park MD. All rights reserved.

45

The bedding was made of either rotten straw or a few dirty, torn blankets. Usually four prisoners shared the *coya*, the bedframe. In reality there were many more, most of the time a dozen. She squeezed up against strangers. Who were those detainees with my mother? How many came back? Did they get along? Did they argue? I learn from Odette Abadi's account, *Land of Distress*, that the women had to remain lying in the same direction or turn together. How did Perla fall asleep? Did she manage to find sleep between the tears, the death rattles? More unanswered questions.

I notice that the kitchen was close to Perla's area. She would go to that kitchen to steal; her route is more concrete for me. It's strange to find this map, so many years later, while doing a search on the Internet, to discover the exact location of the living quarters. The women's quarters were so close to the crematorium. Perla never spoke to me about the odor of burned flesh. Why? She couldn't have forgotten it.

FIG. 10. Women's bunks. Courtesy of the author.

NEXT TO SOPHIE'S tomb, Novalis writes: "Millennia flee to the horizon, like storm clouds." He sees the invisible, the traits of his loved one brought back to life. A boundary no longer exists between life and death. If Friedrich had written these words about Birkenau, they would have had another meaning. Perhaps. It is possible to create poetry out of the worst situations. The sparkling night. That's beautiful. This can describe the night of any camp. *Leaf floating in limitless space, seeks his tree and his place*—how sweet are these verses of Baldur von Schirach, the man who was in charge of the Hitler Youth! Where would it fall, this leaf? Buchenwald . . . that's pretty; it means "the beech tree forest," Birkenau, the "birch prairie." As Ruth Klüger writes in *Refusal to Testify*: "Unknowingly, a person could, while sleepwalking, hum about Birkenau and Buchenwald to the tune of a popular song, and then just as easily come up with some beautiful verse about nature."

And yet, Jean Clair opens *Ordinary Barbarity* with this phrase by Hölderlin: "What remains is what the poet creates." Poetry is still there beyond the ashes; it can still elevate us, make us superhuman. A little farther in, the author writes: "Poetry is the only response to death." Pierre Bertaux, in *Hölderlin or the Time of a Poet*, also points out that "for Hölderlin, poetry is a means of action. . . . He writes to affect the reader, to transform him." For him, it is not a profession, it is a religion. It allows one to return to the original purity of man, that which can make us believe in humanity, a humanity after Auschwitz.

My book is transforming me as I write it. Four Friedrichs will forever be with me. Schlegel, Novalis, Hölderlin, and Caspar David.

FOR THE *KAPOS*, the *Kommandoführers*, everything had to be efficient, logical, tidy; one had to keep moving (*Bewegung*). Where does this necessity come from, this permanent thrusting forward and leitmotif?

Julien always needs novelty. Everything interests him only for a second: a stuffed animal, a piece of paper, an old cell phone, a block, a square piece of wood. He touches everything, puts everything he can in his mouth, and then abandons his discovery with disdain. We adults too always need a new book, a new movie, new music, a new trip, a new love affair, a new delicacy, new earthly nourishment. Attracted by the Planet Variety, we drift away from the feeling of the moment, from profound pleasure, from the very enjoyment of being alive.

FIG. 11. Auschwitz. Courtesy of the author.

I learned by chance that Perla was part of the 77th convoy, the last one sent to Auschwitz on July 31, 1944. The convoy brought 1,300 deportees, 300 of whom were children from the Jewish boarding school in La Varenne. Seven hundred and twenty-five were gassed upon arrival. More than half of them. Extermination was the priority. On that day she heard the endless noise of metal wheels. If it had been a few days later, she might never have been deported to Silesia. She would surely have lived differently: carefree, unscathed. She would have met another man, and I would not have been born. That's all that I know about my mother's deportation. I feel so alone when I immerse myself in her suffering. What exactly did Perla pass on to me, from her flesh to mine? I don't really know. If I hammer away at writing, it's in an attempt to lighten my mind, get rid of my baggage. No matter how hard I try to go back in time, I learn no additional clues about her. From the Memorial to the newspaper of the Friends of Deportees, I obtain no new information. I just sent an email to the Auschwitz museum. They informed me that the Nazis destroyed the majority of the camp's archives. Everything remains unclear. Is there nothing left to find out? She only left me a few clues. Our life lines are not linear. They follow unpredictable paths, take inexplicable turns, are at the whim of personality and events. I want to delve into my memory until no more black ink remains. Human beings, even those closest to us, even our relatives, allow us to see only a part of themselves.

I TAKE A flight to Kraków. I am afraid of having an accident. How ironic it would be to disappear on my way there, sixty years later. I then take a chartered tourist bus and reach that place I have so often imagined, about which I have read so many descriptions. Is it not insane to come here? Perla also made the journey with former deportees. What good can come from this trip? I am not here out of voyeurism. I have another idea in mind. I cross the notorious gate with the inscription *Arbeit macht frei*. I pass before a series of blocks and find myself on a deserted square. There, I take a box of matches and burn my manuscript. I want to be done with this useless literature, this damned past. My book is of no interest. I decide to eliminate it at all cost, at the place of its conception, from where it emerged. While I have been writing, others have had the time to accomplish thousands of heroic acts, to fight barbarity in a concrete way.

FIG. 12. Auschwitz. Courtesy of the author.

I must disengage from this book and finally find some freedom. "You are pathetic, pretentious before these millions of dead, these children who are gone forever! I have lived far too long as a poetic prisoner. Away with you, hack writing! Go to the black hole of humanity, absolute nothingness. Finish your path here; yes, it's for the best! I must become like Wilhelm, useful to society, instead of losing myself in useless writing and thoughts."

The hero of Goethe's famous novel, *Wilhelm Meister's Apprenticeship*, does not want to assume his father's profession as a well-to-do shopkeeper. He leaves his family for a career in theater. He discovers the bohemian life of itinerant actors. After numerous adventures, he renounces this vocation, becomes a surgeon, gets married, and discovers fatherhood. It is now his turn to watch over his son's education. Wilhelm thus progressively finds his path, his truth, his worth. In the beginning, man strays, not knowing how to choose the right road to achieve his goal.

Thanks to his apprenticeship, he chooses a well-practiced craft rather than the marginality of artists. One must learn to live for others by dedicating oneself to a purposeful activity. A man cannot be happy as long as he does not master his infinite desires and does not know his own limits.

No, it's not possible. I awake with a start. I am coming out of a bad dream. I don't want to commit myself to the path of renouncement like Wilhelm Meister. Besides, in the camps, *Meister* referred to the project managers, vicious little bosses who supervised the work of the detainees! My manuscript is still here, lying calmly beside my computer. What good would come from destroying it?

OTTO AMBROS, one of the directors of IG Farben, declared in 1942 that Auschwitz lent itself quite well to the installation of chemical factories. The *Interessengemeinschaft Farbenindustrie* became, at that moment, the largest conglomerate of that era for the manufacturing of synthetic products of all types, notably Zyklon B. In the center bordering Birkenau, they manufactured, among other things, rubber. The factory at Auschwitz was three times larger than the camp itself.

At the end of the war, the gigantic company was divided into several groups: Agfa, BASF, Bayer, Hoechst . . . for that matter, I have probably unknowingly bought one of their products! Twenty-four managers of the group were condemned at Nuremberg for crimes against humanity, but how many men and women implicated in the final solution continued to conduct business? I know that my mother worked in a factory, that she sometimes even secretly washed her clothes in the chemical solutions. Was it in the IG Farben factory? Yet one more secret. Why did we never speak of it? Perla managed to cover her traces, to tell me the least possible. She never compelled me to ask her a lot of questions. Was it out of decency? She certainly took many of her secrets with her.

ANNIE ERNAUX WROTE: "Mom is dead, I will never be able to write these words in a work of fiction." To tell the truth, I don't exactly know what it is I am writing. It's not a novel, it's not a journal, it's not an autofiction. So what is it? "I" is a shadow. Literature is the portrait of shadows. Those of Manon, Julien, and myself wander around in my book. We appear otherwise in real life.

Montaigne Avenue. Her quiet agony continued over numerous years. Entombed in her silence, at the heart of this luxurious avenue, at the end of a marble entrance, at the end of a lush courtyard. Her silence hung heavily on our traditional Sunday night dinners and immersed us in unspoken sadness. At the table there reigned a definite "I have too much to say," "I have nothing to say," or "I don't know what to say."

Sometimes in the street I see a silhouette that resembles her, a gait, hair. I believe it for several seconds. Images abound in my mind, but I barely have the time to receive a few flashes in my head before I realize it's a mirage. I would like to call her to say that life is beautiful, that Julien is beautiful but not easy to live with either, and especially to tell her that I miss her, but I inherited her silence, her silence in perpetuity. She is the soul of my soul, the tears of my tears. I see her again mending a button on one of my jackets. What is more beautiful than a mother who sews for her child? Perla, bent over, concentrating on her work. I watch you cut the thread with your teeth. I watch you manipulate the needle. What a beautiful image! Perla, you caressed me tenderly, kissed me as only a mother knows how, with all of her kindness. You dressed, undressed, fed, and put me to sleep, and in one instant everything was gone.

THE YELLOW STAR, we didn't even speak of that. Did she wear it? Did someone denounce her or was she simply arrested by chance? Was she watched for a long time by the Gestapo? At Drancy, the camp, it was the French who handed her over to the Germans. Our country had been quite happy to engage her brother Mayer to fight on the front lines. He succumbed at the very beginning of the war, "died for France." The official letter reached my grandfather's house on May 16, 1941: "I have the honor of announcing to you that I have been notified of the death of soldier Mayer." What honor are we talking about? I look at the photocopy of that letter. Another letter, this time from the Red Cross, provides a few more details. Soldier Mayer, twenty-two years old, of the 13th squadron, passed away in Beuvardes at the intersection of the roads for Fresnes and Fère-en-Tardenois, on June 9th, 1940. I would have loved to have known him, this uncle. I only have a few photos of him, one with his uniform. It seems to have come from another time.

THE WAVES OF sea foam are henceforth far away and no longer break on the cliffs. The light on the bay lies suspended somewhere between gold and silver. Several sailboats have stopped on the calm waters. A grandfather, a man, and a child play on the shore under the setting sun, and the ships seem to smile at this moment. I contemplate this peaceful painting, *The Stages of Life*. Would we have arrived on islands of sheer happiness?

I feel like abandoning the painful shores of my past, my reflections, and like Ardinghello, mooring along serene land. Exceptionally gifted but stunted by all of life's daily annoyances, the hero of Wilhelm Heinse's novel dreams of

FIG. 13. *The Stages of Life*, by Caspar David Friedrich (oil on canvas, ca. 1835). BAL 824. Museum der Bildenden Kunste, Leipzig, Germany. © Bridgeman Images.

building his own domain, far from people and continents. Struggling, he overcomes all trials in order to live his dream and fully assume his superiority. Accomplished—painter, poet, musician, handsome as Apollo, knowledgeable athlete—he is a relentless seducer. In Rome, he apprentices as a painter and is filled with admiration for Raphael's work. He has numerous love affairs until the day he meets the perfect woman, the one who responds to all of his pleasures, both of body and mind. He brings her to the Fortunate Isles. He creates a world of his own, thus ending his existence as a Casanova or Don Juan, becoming a governor, artist, hedonist, humanist, and mystic. Under the spell of this utopia, I imagine the journeys, the scenery, the seasons that await me. I need to separate myself from the world, finally find detachment.

Manon and I try to live a few moments of beauty. We feel good standing before that soothing Mediterranean. Dazzled, we watch the sunsets from the heights of the village of Oia on Santorini Island. Time seems to stand still. I am more serene before this enchanting scenery, caressed by my wife. After these few days of bliss, we visit the Acropolis, that promised land that so inspired the poets who formed the Athenaeum. It is here that I abruptly learn that André has passed away in the midst of the Parisian summer. In a hotel in Athens, when I pick up my phone to talk to my father, there is no answer. At ten o'clock, André must be taking his usual stroll around his athletic club at the Bois de Boulogne. I try again at eight p.m., still no answer. Ten p.m. André must have gone to dinner unexpectedly with his friend Michel. Eleven p.m., still no one. The night becomes interminable. At eight in the morning, the caretaker finally answers: "I have some bad news to tell you," she announces. An entire part of my life has forever vanished. There will be no more frivolity, lightness. There will always be this ringing in the void.

The bare trees moan at first light. Their groans congeal in their branches. Their trunks resemble columns. Abandoned crosses tilt forward, skimming the ground. In the golden sky, the sun, barely visible, remains indifferent. I look at the painting *The Abbey in the Oakwood* with infinite sadness. Months of pain merge together. This painting is

FIG. 14. *Abbey in the Oakwood*, by Caspar David Friedrich (oil on canvas, 1810). BAL 5335. Schloss Charlottenburg, Berlin, Germany. © Bridgeman Images.

the cover of Georg Büchner's novel *Lenz*. After my father's death I return to the Basque Country. I feel a profound need to walk on the mountainous summits. Leaning against an oak tree, I search the sky for the slightest ray of light that might outline a face; I watch for signs, a gesture, a smile. I find nothing. I have the feeling of having slipped behind a veil into a world of fog, dust, and ash, of having entered into the painting *Sturm und Drang*. I don't want to follow in the footsteps of Lenz, who was unable to rid himself of his pain while walking in the mountains. Before hopelessness sets in, I sense that I have to quickly flee this state of mind, return to my child's smiles.

THERE WAS NO goodbye, no transfer of power. There was only desolation. Funeral parlor, morgue, center for disease control, these are the terms with which I am becoming familiar. For some time I have been living in the world of the dead, which has its own institutions even within the world of the living. With this most recent shock, I lose Perla all over again. I can't take any more of this interminable mourning. I must learn to live in the present, knowing all the while that everything becomes tomb and dust. I don't know, however, the extent to which I am only at the beginning of a long tunnel. The worst is still to come. Perla and André are, from this point forward, beneath the ground. The apartment where they spent more than forty years of life together is still there, silent. It hasn't changed. I witness the ballet of funeral directors, police, cleaners, auctioneers, movers, and landlords who want their signature in order to release the property. I understand quickly that for these people my suffering has absolutely no importance. The misfortune of some leads to the fortune of others. Death allows a multitude of professions to exist. Nothing is lost. Each one demands his recompense.

And then, thankfully, there are things that cannot be taken. These letters, these announcements, these photographs, the memories of trips. I know every nook of this four-room apartment by heart. I must keep, give away, sell, or discard. The choice is difficult. Time accelerates the rhythm of the decisions to be made. I'll keep the essential for the rest of my life. Several books will find a home in my study. I scatter objects and paintings along my way like precious gems that from now on are going to take on a different meaning in the lives of others. I want to rid myself quickly of a material past that has become much too cumbersome, not physically but emotionally. I am familiar with everything in this dwelling. In emptying it, I am at once assassinating both my childhood and my adolescence. One shouldn't rub salt in the wound for too long a time. No matter how much Manon and I try to air out the rooms, abandon them to the four winds, nothing can be done. The smell of an entire life stagnates, persists. I walk through the vestiges of my past trying to hold back my tears. The inanimate objects remind me that my parents will never again return within these walls. I must face the facts: I am in the process of burying forty years of love. I find a folder. With his most beautiful script, André wrote the name "Perla." Written below, "notes for a book." Inside, I read several phrases thrown quickly on paper. The words are barely visible: "I am trying to live without you, Perla, my love. I am on a life raft, the storm rages within me . . ." Too bad he didn't finish it. I think he was never very far from me, inspiring me to write my own.

This painful period of sorting continues for a long time. I uncover a destructive process similar to my path of rebirth. Lighten my life: this has become my one mantra. I want to distance myself from everything that is not essential. Purge my house, my mind, my relationships, my activities, my shelves, my schedule. Everything is fair game for elimination, for destruction: everything not of primary importance must be wiped off the map, thrown out as soon as possible. I rid myself of books and discs that mean little to me, of everything that prevents me from existing. I wage war against the superfluous. I don't realize that, even if my will to do this is very deep, my battle will continue months and months . . . years even. My trash cans fill from one day to the next with kilos of paper and plastic.

SEARCHLIGHTS SWEEPING RED brick blocks with their despotic light; rain, snow, hail, wind striking hopeless bodies; those intertwined corpses; those inexorably aimed submachine guns; that watchtower and that barbed wire in the frozen expanse; that gate crossed by rail ties—nothing can be done. I cannot erase all of these images. Perla, how could they have done this? I search for something against which to compare what happened to her, but nothing suffices. I will never feel what she experienced there.

Why seek to understand the incomprehensible? As Joseph Bialot insists, Auschwitz can be defined neither by words, nor images, nor sounds. The barrier is insurmountable. Very often, the links of communication between survivors and their children are broken. For them, this period in history is "an implausible reality."

FIG. 15. Auschwitz. Courtesy of the author.

It will always remain that incommunicable, inconceivable thing that Perla dragged around behind her. I can only be a spectator. On each page of witness testimonies, I search for a clue about my mother. In *It's in Winter That the Days Get Longer*, Joseph Bialot evokes an ephemeral Perla, seductive, with a Red Cross insignia on her blouse. How many Perlas were there in the camp? Is he talking about my mother? I don't believe so. This woman, sadly, must have disappeared over there. Why am I still there, pursuing a fleeting shadow that vanished long ago into the corridors of history? As of now, the majority of survivors are dead. I want to stop this hollow quest. In the end, Perla was right to protect me, to tell me the least possible. Useless to continue adding to the horror of horrors, to discover anecdotes that could only do me harm. I no longer wish to go back in time. Everyone must learn to overcome the past (*Vergangenheitsbewältigung*). The length of the word in German illustrates the difficulty of the task.

I LOOK AGAIN at our photos. They are black and whites. I am a newborn: Perla has a happy look on her face, eyes that shine. I am in her arms, swaddled, on the patio of a cabin in Megève. The mountain in the distance is majestic. I am one year old, I am taking a shower, I'm laughing. I'm five years old. She still holds me as tightly in her arms. The smile is still there. The eyes shine slightly less. We pass to color photos. She holds me by the hand in a house in Le Touquet. She is helping me climb onto a wall. I am looking at the sky, worried, afraid. I am twelve years old. I am kissing her on the mouth on a beach in Cannes. André didn't like this. But it's cute. I have my head on her breast. There is sunlight in her gaze. Her skin is soft. The world could have exploded. No matter. We were so happy. I'm past thirty years old. From this point on, she has her mouth open as if she is having trouble breathing. Even though everything in the photo is frozen, immobile, I still see how slowly she walks, how poorly, unstable. She no longer lifts her feet. I learn about her travels with André. You can tell that these trips bore her. She accompanies her husband out of kindness. Morocco, Malta, Martinique, Africa . . . the landscapes file by, change, but the face, no. Sometimes, she appears happy again. It's unclear why. They say everyone needs a change of scenery, but the scenery doesn't change her. Neither do the spa treatments. Against the backdrops of the sea, ancient towns, fishing ports, boats, plains, the desert, trees, flowers, her expression is practically always the same. Perla is walking, dragging her feet on the sidewalks or in the sand. Beautiful hotels, vistas. Nothing works. In this image, Perla finally seems lighter. Behind her, rose petals reflect her newly rediscovered joy, and then, suddenly, photographs of those bouquets on her tomb, those sprays of flowers sent by dear friends. André took pictures of them as well. Everything is now put away in a box. I chose a very colorful one. It's a little less sad that way. An entire life in such a small amount of cardboard. I am older. Again, another one. She is lounging on the sofa. Her head rests against my shoulder. I am happy. I don't even realize it. My mother is still there.

In her journal, *An Interrupted Life*, Etty Hillesum, a young Dutch Jew who disappeared at Auschwitz, complained before her deportation of a bizarre, creative, diabolical restlessness that unremittingly consumed her mind. That restlessness: it was necessary to find—at all costs—a way of channeling it. Despite writing about it, she did not manage to rid herself of her internal turmoil, to come up with the exact form of expression needed. Isn't it impossible to try to summarize one's life on paper, to enclose it within a volume? How can one hope to contain the world within a few formulaic expressions? The writer Ernst Jünger compares literature to the "house of being." It allows one to regain one's "native land," the *Heimat*. Perla's land, her *Heimat*, her original homeland, what was it really?

THE TREES IN the Pantin cemetery seem to beckon me. They connect me with my parents, of whom nothing remains except names engraved in gold letters on a gray marble tombstone. What joy those phone calls brought, even when there was nothing to say, apart from communicating the good fortune of just being there, all together! That voice, so present, so precious, its magical tone: those wonderful words bringing news of an ordinary day, I still want to enjoy them. I am writing these words in the sitting room of the exercise club where André spent some of his last hours. During the heatwave, it was a cool haven for him, thanks to the air conditioning. I might be sitting in the same chair he did. There is still a bit of his soul in the worn leather. I scan the air in this room in order to sense whether any of his last thoughts still remain. There is nothing. Not a word, not a syllable. I will no longer speak with André. He will no longer tell me anything about Perla.

How has this headlong rush helped me, this perpetual hustle and bustle, this *Bewegung*, this pursuit of a professional career that never ends? Now that I look back at the road behind me, I see derailments, mistakes, misunderstandings. It's possible to think that the arrival of a child will erase the death of a parent or, at least, will ease the sorrow. Such is not the case. The loss of a loved one sets your soul on fire, burns it. Comments from those who have never lost anyone graze over without touching you. The disappearance of a parent is a personal affliction. One part of your soul is blown away, another remains here on earth, fragmented, impenetrable. Yet we all must continue to move forward in order to not be struck down by our words and regrets. "Young man, move forward, but don't be in too much of a hurry." This is what I would like to say to Julien. "Don't worry about us, live your life, but listen to us, look at us really closely, if only for a few instants. We will not always be here. Be wholly present with us; forget yourself if only for a moment. Your awareness will allow you always to preserve this magical thread that connects us; Keep moving forward. Death does not wait." This is what an incessant voice deep within keeps saying to me. I hope that Julien will hear it sooner than I did. To enjoy life totally and completely, you must never forget the presence of loved ones. Once you are permeated by this idea, you are ready to face existence so as to live a life of love, to discover love in death. "It was the thought of death, rooted deep within him, that multiplied each of his joys and mollified each of his sorrows. The sensuous idea of all things ending caused him to concentrate all of his life force on the present moment, and in one day, he lived more than others would in a year." This is where I want to stop, declares Andreas Hartknopf, the hero of Karl Philipp Moritz's book. This is also where I want to stop. At forty years old, Andreas returns to the home he left twenty years earlier. Blacksmith by trade, he decided over time to ceaselessly elevate his mind by practicing multiple disciplines. During his apprenticeship years, he advanced in the fields of theology, astronomy, music, poetry. However, what distinguishes this novel from all other coming-of-age stories is that it is principally one long allegory about death.

This was what I was missing since infancy: an understanding of this death. I was poorly prepared for it. Only its visits, its integration into our lives, can mature us. Before learning the lesson that it alone can teach us, without the firm understanding that it is there, that it lies in wait for us, we view the present moment as if it were a puppet show, an illusion.

Some German words are impossible to translate. *Sehnsucht* is perhaps the best example. Dictionaries may well

FIG. 16. *Morning in the Giant Mountains*, by Caspar David Friedrich (oil on canvas). BAL 90204. State Hermitage Museum, St. Petersburg, Russia. © Bridgeman Images.

associate it with nostalgia, languor, melancholia, but no term can define it precisely for us, as it refers as much to the past as to the future. Indeed, it evokes a yearning for a place beyond time and space. We feel it most strongly when, from the top of a mountain, our soul contemplates the infinite landscape. Tranquility and purity fill our being. *Sehnsucht* is what stirs the poet indescribably when he feels connected to something beyond. For a few moments, internal beauty becomes one with the world around it. The artist thus tries to inject into a poem, book, or painting this *Sehnsucht* that is so difficult to communicate. He who contemplates it, listens to it, must be stirred by the same internal beauty in order to find this wholeness.

I SOMETIMES VISIT her in that garden so distant from our day-to-day reality, in that islet of stone and green space, scarcely a few meters from the city made of asphalt and glass. There is but one gate to enter. A smiling guard allows me to pass. There are six plots in our family crypt. After Perla's, André's, his father's, his mother's, and Nacha's, only one remains. Mine. My parents are separated from me by light-years and yet, in my mind, they were never as present as they are now. Henceforth they will reside at the end of an alley called "Chênes-de-Rome." It's a beautiful address.

I was in the habit of giving my mother roses in threes, her favorite number. I continue, in the most profound silence, to plant them at the foot of her unassuming marble tombstone. Each time I open a book about Auschwitz, I remind myself that I was lucky to live with Perla. I think about all those children who lost their parents there. Even coming to this cemetery is a privilege. I think about all of the unburied dead. I just reread Ruth Klüger's testimony. For her, one shouldn't confuse statistics with predestination. If survivors are still around, it is but a question of luck. Luck, predestination, both still unknowns in my mind—I, who was born lucky.

I keep a glossy photo of her in my wallet. The anguished smile of her final years. Why is absence always necessary to amplify love? I return to that bench at the Kremlin-Bicêtre. In the courtyard of this hospital, other lives, other stories are still unfolding. Years have passed. Despair came to visit me, but suffering purifies us. It distances us too. It forces us to leave the obscure realm of a self that believes in its omnipotence. It forces us to wake up and realize that life no longer has the same meaning. It separates some people, brings others together. It reveals to us the inadequacy of our actions. It prompts the need for writing, which further increases this confinement. It plants a new urgency in us. It forces us to grow, to enter into a never-ending spiral that abruptly changes color. Suddenly, we become more tolerant; we realize that we are not the only ones suffering, that we should be wary of appearances so that we can finally return to the world.

FIG. 17. Park bench. Courtesy of the author.

Silence is powerful, timeless, reassuring. I tell her that I finished our book. She responds, "Forget about it, be happy, as I always wanted, even if I didn't know how to express it." I promise her I will do everything in my power to do so. We talk about Julien, who exudes enthusiasm. My every moment is swathed in his enchanting laugh. Little by little, by renouncing material abundance, I find once more the clarity that had been lying dormant within my being for a long time. It slowly brings back joyfulness, month after month: like the crest of a wave, my tears form a sea foam of beauty. These pages created out of sorrow will become a joyous book. Manon is taking care of me. Everything is for the best. Perla, I will always wear a backpack, that of a child leaving for the school of life. You still fill it. A mother, in fact, never dies.

CPSIA information can be obtained
at www.ICGtesting.com
Printed in the USA
LVOW11s0037030817
543574LV00003B/258/P